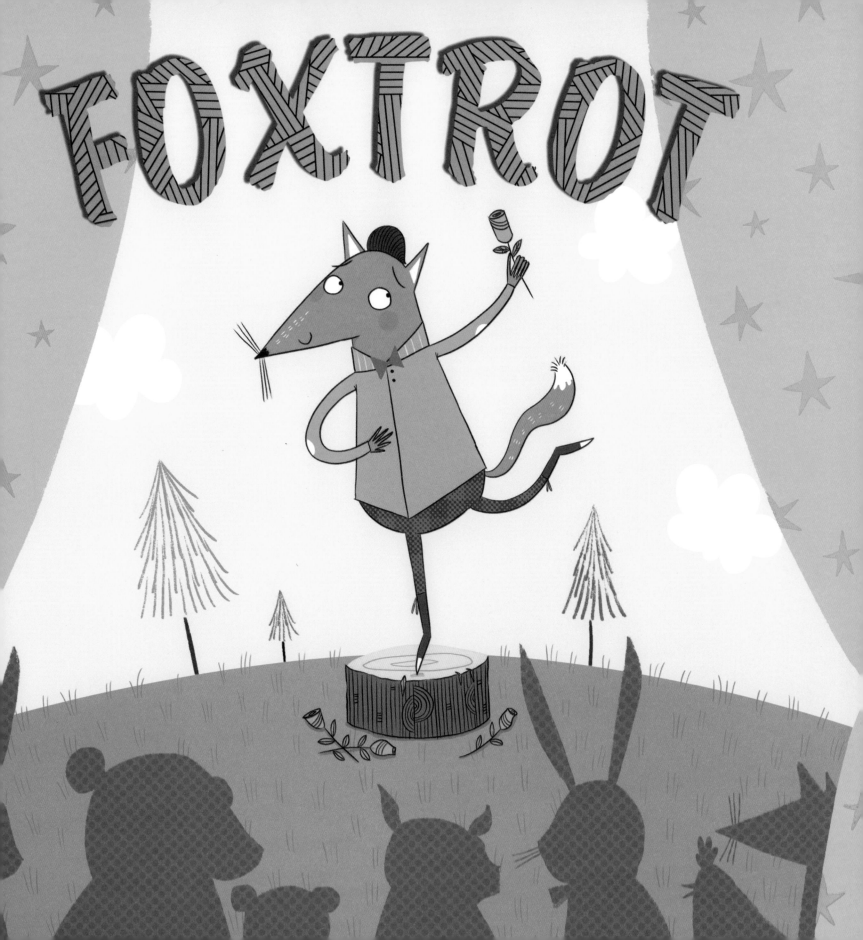

little bee books
An imprint of Bonnier Publishing Group
853 Broadway, New York, New York 10003
Copyright © 2015 by Becka Moor
First published in Australia by The Five Mile Press.
This little bee books edition, 2015.
All rights reserved, including the right of reproduction in whole
or in part in any form. LITTLE BEE BOOKS is a trademark of
Bonnier Publishing Group, and associated colophon is a trademark
of Bonnier Publishing Group.
Manufactured in China 0315 HH
First Edition 2 4 6 8 10 9 7 5 3 1
Library of Congress Control Number: 2015934155
ISBN 978-1-4998-0132-3

www.littlebeebooks.com
www.bonnierpublishing.com

FOXTROT

by Becka Moor

little bee books

FOXTROT loved to dance.

He DANCED out of bed and into the bathroom.

He BOOGIED while he combed his whiskers

and TWIRLED as he brushed his teeth.

He DANCED as he dressed and did SPLITS as he put on socks.

He JUMPED and JIVED and swung and swayed until his disco clock told him it was time for breakfast.

He **TANGOED** with his toast and **MAMBOED** with his marmalade.
There was nothing Foxtrot could not foxtrot to.
Life was music to his ears.

Unfortunately for Foxtrot, not everybody felt the same.

His dancing feet caused MAYHEM in town. They got in everyone's way and brought traffic to a standstill.

They caused **CALAMITIES** in stores, knocking things over and annoying all the customers.

They caused pandemonium at parties and CHAOS everywhere he went.

Eventually, Foxtrot's friends decided they just HAD to tell him how much trouble his dancing feet were causing.

Poor Foxtrot didn't understand. He
thought everyone loved his DANCING!

But how wrong he was.
His BOOGYING had to stop. But how?

His friend Rory tried tying Foxtrot's shoelaces together.

But Foxtrot couldn't stay still for very long
and kept **FALLING** over.

Bernard the Bear stuck Foxtrot's feet to the floor with Mr. B's super strong and STICKY honey.

But Foxtrot got LONELY standing all by himself.

Eventually, Foxtrot decided that enough was enough.
There must be something else he would enjoy
as much as he enjoyed dancing.

So he tried rock climbing.
   But Foxtrot soon discovered that he was
                    PETRIFIED of heights.

He tried acting, but he kept forgetting his lines.

Poor Foxtrot got **BOOED** off the stage.

He even tried drag-racing,
but it was far too fast
and made him feel all WOOZY.

All Foxtrot wanted to do was DANCE.

One morning, Foxtrot dragged himself out of bed and shuffled into the bathroom.

He **SIGHED** while combing his whiskers and **HUFFED** as he put on socks. He heaved and stumbled and moaned as he slowly got ready for breakfast.

As Foxtrot nibbled on his dry toast, he noticed something out of the corner of his eye.

It was a picture of him and his dance teacher. Mrs. Flamenco had grown too old to run her school, but Foxtrot missed it very much.

Just as he was about to head back to bed, Foxtrot had a BRILLIANT idea.

"I will run the school!" he said, much to his friends' bewilderment.

"Then I can **DANCE** as much as I like, whenever I like!"

His friends weren't so sure that
Foxtrot's plan would work.

Still, they decided to lend a helping hand.

After a fresh coat of paint, Foxtrot's school was ready to open.
He couldn't wait to show it off.

Foxtrot held a **HUGE** opening ceremony and invited
everyone he knew to come and see his new dance school.

Foxtrot's friends were impressed. And when they saw how happy dancing made Foxtrot, they all signed up for his classes. Soon, everyone learned to LOVE dancing.

But no one could DANCE quite like Foxtrot.
And I don't think anyone ever will.